Strange
Journey Back

Strange
Journey Back

Written by Paul McCusker

Illustrated by Karen Loccisano

PUBLISHING

Colorado Springs, Colorado

STRANGE JOURNEY BACK

Library of Congress Cataloging-in-Publication Data

McCusker, Paul, 1958-
   Strange journey back / Paul McCusker ; illustrations by Karen Loccisano.
     p.   cm. — (Adventures in Odyssey ; 1)
   Summary: Distressed by his parents' separation, Mark tries to go back in time to set things right and discovers that some changes are unavoidable.
   ISBN 1-56179-101-6 (pbk.) :
   [1. Divorce—Fiction. 2. Time travel—Fiction.] I. Loccisano, Karen, ill.   II. Title.
III. Series: McCusker, Paul, 1958-
Adventure in Odyssey ; 1
PZ7M47841635St   1992
[Fic]—dc20

                                   91-8
                                   CIP
                                   AC

Published by Focus on the Family Publishing, Colorado Springs, CO 80995.

Distributed in the U.S.A. and Canada by Word Books, Dallas, Texas.

Editors: Sheila Cragg and Janet Kobobel
Designer: Sherry Nicolai Russell
Cover and Interior Illustrations: Karen Loccisano

Adventures in Odyssey Radio Drama
(A Focus on the Family Production)
Creators: Phil Lollar, Steve Harris
Executive Producer: Chuck Bolte
Scriptwriters: Phil Lollar, Paul McCusker
Production Engineers: Dave Arnold, Bob Luttrell

Printed in the United States of America

    97 98 99/10 11

To Nancy L. Freed.
It is an honor to be your son.

The Adventures in Odyssey novels takes place in a time period prior to the beginning of the audio or video series. That is why some of the characters from those episodes don't appear in these stories — they don't exist yet.

Contents

CHAPTER ONE

A Letter and a Mission

Mark Prescott walked down the sidewalk with grim determination. In his hand, he clutched an envelope. In his heart, he carried a single desire: More than anything else, he wanted things to be the way they used to be.

He wanted things to be the way they were earlier in the spring before his dad left them; before Mark and his mom moved from his neighborhood and friends in Washington, D.C.; before they came to this little town called Odyssey; before . . . before, well, before everything went wrong.

No matter what Mark was doing or thinking about, that one desire stayed with him—to change things back.

He didn't have time for the hot June day or the gentle

breeze that whispered the first secrets of summer. He was on a mission. He had written a letter to his father, and he had to get it mailed.

Mark walked quickly, glancing from one side to the other. The tarred street to his left looked like a steaming black river. To his right, the last Victorian house slipped away like the caboose on a long train. Odyssey Elementary School slid into view. It would be Mark's school in the fall, if he was still living in Odyssey, if he couldn't make things the way they used to be.

He was looking ahead when his attention was suddenly drawn to the playground. Two kids were wrestling on the grass. Next to them, a couple of bikes lay like crippled horses that had fallen to the ground.

"Ouch," cried one of the wrestlers.

"Cut it out," hollered the second kid.

The one with sandy hair, dirty jeans and T-shirt sat triumphantly on the chest of the darker-haired one.

"Say you're sorry," the victor kept shouting.

"Ow! Get off!" the dark-haired kid whined.

Mark felt sorry for the kid on the bottom. He knew what it was like to be bullied. One time Cliff Atkinson sat on Mark's chest at recess and tried to take his lunch money. Just as Mark was about to give in, Lee Brooks grabbed Cliff and pulled him off so Mark could defend himself. Lee did crazy things like that. From then on, Lee had become his best friend.

Remembering how Lee had rescued him, Mark started across the field toward the fighters. Maybe he could help. Maybe he would make a new friend like Lee Brooks. His pace quickened to a run as he shoved the letter into his back pocket.

"Say you're sorry," the sandy-haired kid shouted again.

"Let me go!" the darker-haired kid on the bottom cried.

Mark locked his arms around the one on top and pulled hard.

"Hey, stop it!" The kid cried out with surprise.

The one on the bottom jumped up like a freed animal. His dark hair was matted to his sweaty forehead; his face was dirty and streaked with tears. A drop of blood bubbled out of his nose. He was taller than any of them.

"Hah," the boy shouted, as if he had gotten free without any help. "You're in big trouble. I'm going to get you for this!"

The boy pulled his bike upright, climbed on it and pedaled off without even saying thanks to Mark.

The sandy-haired kid broke loose from Mark's grip and turned on him. Bright blue eyes shone with fury, and the face contorted into an expression that could have withered houseplants.

Mark gave a startled gasping sound and exclaimed, "You're a girl!"

CHAPTER TWO

Unwanted Changes

The girl threw a punch at Mark. As her hand flew past his face, he stepped backward, tripped and fell. Catlike, she pounced onto his chest and pinned his arms to the ground.

"Do you know what you did?" she screamed. "I waited the whole school year to get Joe! He picked on me. Called me bad names. And just when I—" She let out an angry huffing sound, swallowed and then asked in a hoarse growl, "Do you know what you did?"

Mark considered wrestling his way out from under her. He knew he could, but he didn't. Instead, he said calmly, "Get off my chest."

"You ruined it! You ruined everything! Joe Devlin's

5

been needing a good pounding all year."

"I'm sorry," Mark said. "I didn't know."

"You're sorry!" she shouted.

"Yeah," Mark answered quietly.

She looked puzzled. "You're sorry?"

"Yeah."

She blinked a couple of times. Her weight on Mark's chest lessened as she climbed off.

"Oh," she said and sat on the grass next to him. She looked confused.

Mark propped himself up on his elbows and took a deep breath.

"Well . . . ," the girl fumbled, "you should be sorry."

Mark got up and pulled the letter out of his pocket. It was wrinkled and sweaty. *It doesn't look too bad,* he thought.

He turned back to the girl. "I have to leave," he said and started to walk across the field toward the post office.

By the time Mark reached the sidewalk, she was at his side walking her bike.

"I don't know you," she announced. "You're new in Odyssey, right?"

"Yeah." Mark picked up his pace.

"You live in old lady Schaeffer's house, right?"

Mark nodded. *Old lady,* Mark mused. *Is that what they called her?*

"Old lady" Schaeffer was Mark's grandmother, his

mom's mom. The house had been his grandmother's until she died a couple of years ago and left everything in a will to Mark's mom. He hadn't known his grandmother very well, only through the usual Christmas or birthday cards.

"You're there with your mom, right?"

Mark wished this girl would leave him alone. She asked too many questions. Sooner or later, she would ask about his father.

"Look," Mark said, suddenly stopping. "I said I was sorry for ruining your fight. But I have to go. Nice to meet you." He took longer strides, hoping she wouldn't follow anymore.

The bike rattled behind him. *Maybe she'll climb on it and ride away,* he thought.

But she was at his side again. "Are you going to Whit's End? Looks like you're headed that way. I'm going to Whit's End, too."

"I'm going to the post office. I don't know what a Whit's End is."

"You don't know about Whit's End? Guess you've been hiding since you moved here."

"We've been busy. We had to unpack lots of boxes," Mark said defensively.

"Oh. Well, Whit's End is the best place to go in all of Odyssey! It's kind of an ice-cream shop, but it's also got a bunch of inventions and displays and . . ." she paused. "You'll just have to see it. I'll take you after we go to the post office."

After we go to the post office? Mark didn't like the sound of it. His mission didn't include a strange girl.

"But I . . . ," he stopped. He could be rude and tell her to get lost, but his mom had taught him better. "Okay," he finally said.

The rest of the walk to downtown Odyssey took only five minutes. It could have been five hours. Except to tell her his name when she asked, Mark never got a word in because the girl didn't stop talking.

She told him that her name was Patti Eldridge, and then she went on to say, "I like to do a lot of things boys usually like, but the kids make fun of me because I'm girl. And Whit's End is owned by a man named John Avery Whittaker who used to be a teacher, but he quit because he likes to invent things for kids. And right before his wife died, she asked him to open a place like Whit's End."

Her sentences never ended; they just kept going with the word "and." Eventually, Mark did what he always did with people who talked a lot. He stopped listening and let his mind drift to other places.

He was in his bedroom again. Not the bedroom at his grandmother's house but *his* bedroom, the real one in Washington, D.C. He was buttoning his shirt, rushing to get ready for school. He was feeling nervous.

In another part of the house, he heard the voices of his mom and dad. Another fight. They seemed to be having more and more of them. Mark suspected they had tried to hide their fights from him, but they couldn't. He heard them in the morning and sometimes late at night. And even when they weren't fighting, he suffered through the silences at mealtimes. He knew what the late hours his dad kept at the office really meant.

He fumbled with the buttons on his shirt and listened to the voices. His name was mentioned. He froze. As the questions sneaked into his mind, he felt like a fist was punching his stomach. They weren't questions like he had on tests. They were more like feelings with question marks at the end of them: Why did his parents have to fight so much? Why did they say his name?

Maybe he was doing something to make them fight. Maybe it was because he had woken up late for school again. Maybe he had left his shoes in the middle of the kitchen again. Maybe. . . maybe . . . it was his fault. Maybe that's why they didn't fight around him, so he wouldn't hear their list of terrible things he had done to make them fight.

The voices reached a peak and stopped. It was as if a bell had rung, sending the fighters to their corners after another round.

Mark heard a soft shuffle of feet coming up the stairs, down the hall, then stopping at his bedroom door. Mark's dad opened the door and surveyed the room with that familiar frown.

"You're not ready yet," he said. "You want to be late for school again?"

"No, sir," Mark whispered.

"And look at this room. How many times do I have to tell you to clean it?" He shook his head. "Hurry up. Your mother has breakfast waiting for you downstairs."

Mark's father turned and walked away. Shortly afterward, his parents' bedroom door slammed.

In the kitchen his mom didn't say anything. Her eyes were red and wet as she served Mark his breakfast. At one point, she kissed him on the forehead while he ate. She had never done that before. He usually got a kiss on the way out the door. It scared him, and he didn't want to eat anymore.

Finally he put on his coat, grabbed his books and braced himself for the cold morning air. His mom opened the door, leaned down and kissed him again. One of her tears smeared his cheek. And the tear was warm.

Mark stepped out into a nippy February day, thrusting his hands into his coat pockets. He heard the laughter and chatter of the other kids, waiting at the end of the block for the school bus. He wondered if they had mornings like he did. Did their parents have fights before breakfast?

He walked down the front porch steps and glanced back to see his mother close the door. His eyes drifted up to his parents' bedroom window. The curtain moved slightly. For a brief moment, Mark thought he saw his father looking down at him.

Later that afternoon when he came running in after
school, Mark's mom asked him to sit down and listen
carefully. With a quivering voice, she explained that his
dad had left them. She gave some excuses about why he
had. She said he was overworked, they had some problems, and he was confused about things.

But Mark knew the truth. His dad had left because of
him. He had left because Mark had woken up late again,
his room wasn't clean, and his dad couldn't take it anymore. It was Mark's fault.

"There's the post office," Patti said, bringing Mark
back to the present.

Mark rushed into the small brick building, waited in
line, then handed over his letter when it was his turn.

The woman behind the counter smiled wearily and
handed it back. "It's too crumpled," she said. "Put it in
another envelope, honey. You don't want it to get lost, do
you?"

He shook his head and stepped away from the counter.
He had to get the letter to his dad soon.

Outside the post office Mark said to Patti, "I have to go
home right away."

"But we were going to Whit's End."

He started to protest, but she grabbed his sleeve and
tugged him along. "It's right over there," Patti pointed,
"across from McAlister Park. Come on."

He didn't want to be rude; he figured he could escape soon enough. Patti identified the various buildings for Mark as they walked through the park. She showed him the gym, the basketball courts and sports facilities, but he didn't care. Then a different sort of building came into view. It was a large house sitting off by itself, as if it didn't belong.

As he got closer, Mark noticed that the house looked more like a collection of odd-shaped boxes with small, medium and large squares and a rectangular section with windows. It also had a jutting tower and roofs that angled every which way, as if the creator couldn't make up his mind which way to build them.

"That's Whit's End," Patti said.

For a moment Mark was drawn to the strange-looking place. But his mission came to mind again. He didn't want to go to an ice-cream shop. He wanted to go back home. He wanted to get a new envelope and mail the letter to his dad. He wanted to get away from Patti Eldridge, who kept talking even when he stopped listening. Mark was about to tell Patti he had to leave when—BOOM!

CHAPTER THREE

An Explosion at Whit's End

The explosion shook the park, sending echoes through the trees and scattering the birds like a shotgun blast.

"Come on!" Patti said, running toward Whit's End.

By the time they reached the front of the house, a group of kids and a few adults were filing out in orderly fashion. Mark was surprised by the lack of panic. No one was running or screaming. He didn't see any signs of damage. Small clouds of smoke drifted from a basement window.

What a strange place, Mark thought.

"Let's try to get in," Patti said, as they reached the front door. "I want to see what happened."

That was as far as they got.

A man stood in the doorway with a fire extinguisher in his hand. White foam dribbled from the nozzle. "Nothing to worry about," the man announced. "Everything's under control."

His voice was low and fuzzy, and his face was lifted into a large smile. His friendly eyes were bright and clear beneath white bushy eyebrows. The eyebrows matched his mustache and hair, which were thick and untamed.

A fire engine siren screamed in the distance, growing louder as it approached Whit's End from Main Street.

"Completely unnecessary," the man said quietly. Glancing at Mark, he winked.

"What happened, Mr. Whittaker?" Patti asked.

Mr. Whittaker. So this is the one Patti kept talking about. Mark studied the man more seriously.

"A fractured filament," Mr. Whittaker answered. He put down the extinguisher and moved toward the firemen who were jumping off the parked fire engine. Their red helmets and yellow coats looked bright against the green of the park. Whit waved them back. "False alarm, boys. A lot of smoke, that's all."

As the fire chief approached Whit, he ordered the others to go in and check the building.

"The third time in two weeks, Whit," the chief said with a hint of disapproval.

"There's no danger," Whit replied.

"Uh-huh, and what was it *this* time?" the fire chief

asked.

Whit hesitated, his cheeks turning red. "The Imagination Station."

"Huh?"

"A time machine, sort of," Whit offered reluctantly.

A time machine! Mark thought. *Can people really travel through time?*

The fire chief shook his head. "Whit, you're a wacko." Mark heard affection in the man's voice.

Patti leaned toward Mark. "This happens all the time," she whispered. "Whit's always inventing stuff like that."

"Do . . . do the inventions work?" Mark asked.

"Of course!" Patti exclaimed proudly.

Then Mark heard a breathless puffing and a high-pitched voice muttering behind them.

"Uh-oh, here comes Emma Douglas," Patti said with a snicker.

Emma Douglas went straight to Whit. "Mr. Whittaker, please!" she said in a voice full of shaky nerves. "I . . . I told you when I took this job that I'm . . . I'm not very good with . . . with this." She gestured toward Whit's End. A strand of her silver hair came loose from the knot at the back of her head.

Whit smiled, his upper lip disappearing beneath his mustache. Mark thought the smile was reassuring.

"I'm sorry, Emma," Whit said. "I must have made a mistake in my figuring."

Her small hands twisted her apron, as if she were strangling it. "I know you're sorry, Mr. Whittaker, but I . . . I don't think I can stand it anymore. All the tinkering you do, the strange inventions, kids everywhere, loud noises." Emma Douglas caught her breath. "It's too much for me."

Whit pleaded with her. "Emma, give it a little more time."

"I quit, Mr. Whittaker. This minute. This very second. I quit." Emma Douglas turned and went back through the door into Whit's End. The knot of hair at the back of her head bobbed up and down like the tail of a rabbit.

Whit shoved his hands deep into the pockets of his work overalls. "Another one," he said. "That's the third worker I've lost in less than a month."

"No surprise," the fire chief chuckled as he walked away, calling orders to the other firemen to return to the station.

Patti tugged at Whit's sleeve. "Hey, Mr. Whittaker, you have to meet Mark."

Whit turned, giving his full attention to the two of them.

Patti went on, "He's Old Lady Shaef—" she caught herself and started again, "He's Mrs. Shaeffer's grandson. He lives in her house."

"Ah," Whit said. He reached out, took Mark's hand and shook it vigorously. "I knew your grandmother well. A wonderful woman. Are you Julie's son?"

Mark nodded, suddenly shy.

Whit nodded too. "Of course. Your grandmother talked a lot about your family. There were pictures of you in her living room. I remember now."

Mark relaxed. There was something comforting about Whit's knowing who Mark was. He imagined Whit in his grandmother's living room, maybe drinking tea, looking at the family photos and talking about them like old friends would.

"You're better-looking in person." Whit grinned.

"Don't you think so, Patti?" he asked with a nudge.

Patti blushed. "I don't know. I never saw the pictures."

Mark's mind went back to the Imagination Station. He had a lot of questions he was bursting to ask. He had to say something, anything.

"It's very nice to meet you, Mark," Whit said with sincerity. "You should come on into the shop and have a look around. Meanwhile, I need to figure out how I'm going to replace Emma Douglas. Poor woman." He started to walk away from them.

"Mr. Whittaker," Mark blurted suddenly.

Whit stopped and looked back.

Mark didn't know how he was going to say what he wanted to say, but he didn't want to lose the chance to get closer to the Imagination Station. "If you need help, I . . . maybe I could help you."

Whit cocked an eyebrow.

Mark continued, "Maybe until you find someone else, I could be an errand boy or something. You don't even have to pay me."

Whit rubbed his chin thoughtfully. "Hmm, an errand boy."

Mark wanted to say something else, something to convince him, but he couldn't think of anything. His stomach tightened with anticipation.

"Not a bad idea, as a temporary measure."

"It's a great idea," Patti said.

"Come inside, Mark." Whit motioned to him. "I'll call your parents. If it's okay with them, it's okay with me. I could use the help."

Mark's heart raced as they stepped into Whit's End to make the phone call.

CHAPTER FOUR

A Strange Errand

While Whit talked with Mark's mom on the phone, Patti offered to show Mark around the shop. He wanted to tour the place, but more than anything he wanted to see the Imagination Station. He had it all worked out in his mind. If the Imagination Station could really do what they said it could, then Mark might be able to go back in time and change what had happened with his dad. He could make things like they were before his dad left them.

Mark's excitement surged like a current of electricity. He had to find that machine. As Patti guided him through the soda shop, he looked anxiously for something that might resemble an Imagination Station. He noted the snow-white refrigerators and shining silver dispensers. Was the time machine white? Or silver?

Next they went into a room with shelves filled with books. "This is the library," Patti explained.

Mark nodded, imagining that one of the bookcases slid away to reveal a secret room. If one did, Patti didn't give him the chance to see it.

Then she led him into a large auditorium containing a stage for theatrical performances. Looking at Whit's End from the outside, Mark wouldn't have guessed the building was so big.

Upstairs, Patti showed him the county's largest train set. At least that's what the sign beside it declared. The train layout featured scale replicas of classic engines chugging around lifelike hills, valleys and miniature villages.

Kids and adults were everywhere. No one seemed to be concerned about the explosion anymore. Everyone was involved in one game or another. Mark had to admit that Whit's End really was unlike anything he had ever seen before.

They had finished the tour, but Mark hadn't seen anything that looked like an Imagination Station. Patti took him back to the kitchen, where Whit was still talking to Mark's mom on the phone. It was an endless conversation about his grandmother. Finally Whit asked if it was all right for Mark to be his errand boy. The tension was growing in his stomach again.

Whit finally smiled at Mark and gave him the okay sign.

Mark's mind spun with plans. Now that he was an official employee, he hoped Whit would hurry up and show him the Imagination Station.

Whit hung up the phone and slipped behind the ice-cream counter to serve some newly-arrived customers. As he dished out scoops of ice cream, he said, "For now, I'll need you to run some errands for me. I'll show you how to take care of things around the shop later. I don't think it'll be too hard for you."

What about the Imagination Station? Mark wanted to ask. *Where is it? When can I use it? Put the ice cream away and show me how to go back in time!*

Whit glanced at Mark. For a moment he was afraid Whit had read his mind.

"I know what you can do," Whit said. "You can run out to Tom Riley's place and pick up a box for me."

"A box?" Mark asked.

"Not a big one," Whit assured him, lowering his voice to a near-whisper. "It's top secret, though. It's a very important part that I need to get the Imagination Station working again. It broke in the explosion."

"Can I go?" Patti asked.

Mark darted a disapproving look in her direction. He wanted to explain to her that this wasn't a job for a girl.

Top secret stuff was for guys. He was just about to say so, but Whit spoke first.

"Good idea, Patti," Whit said. "You can show Mark how to get to Tom's house."

Patti straightened up proudly. "I know a short cut."

"I figured you would. You'll make a good team." Whit dropped a scoop of vanilla ice cream onto a cone and handed it over the counter to a customer.

Patti tugged at Mark's sleeve. "Let's go."

Mark looked to Mr. Whittaker for any final instructions. Whit smiled at him and nodded. "Tell Tom I sent you. He'll know what to do."

Mark followed Patti outside, but he didn't like having to depend on her. *She's nice enough,* he thought, *but she still talks too much.*

"I know a short cut," she said in the same proud voice she used back at the shop.

"I know, I know," Mark said. He didn't care how they got there. He just wanted to get the missing piece to the Imagination Station.

Patti began to talk again, but Mark's mind wandered off into another daydream. He replayed every detail in his mind of the day his father left, and it gave him new resolve to change things back.

"Hey! Look over there," Patti said.

Mark looked around, surprised to find that he had followed Patti into a clearing. She was pointing to a small grove of trees. Beyond them, Mark saw a large white house and behind it, a barn.

"Are you hungry?" Patti asked.

Mark was, but he shook his head no. "We have to get to Mr. Riley's, Patti."

"I'm hungry," Patti said firmly.

"Okay, okay. You're hungry, but we didn't bring any food."

Patti grinned knowingly. "We didn't need to bring any food. See those trees over there? They have the best apples in the whole county. Come on!"

Before Mark could say anything, Patti dashed off toward the trees. Mark grumbled to himself but ran after her. She was already climbing one of the trees by the time he caught up with her.

"Go on, Mark. Get an apple out of that other tree." Mark hesitated.

"What are you, a chicken? Get yourself an apple! You know you want one."

Mark reached for a lower branch, but a question nagged him. Will the owner mind? He shrugged it off. He didn't want Patti to think he was a coward, so he climbed up into the tree.

Patti was back on the ground by the time he found an apple that looked good enough to eat. She called to him, waving her apple proudly. "I found a big one."

"Hurry up," she said. "You don't want to get caught.

"Caught?" Mark asked, as he snapped off the apple he wanted.

"By the owner," Patti replied. "He's kind of, well, crazy. He gets real mad when kids climb his trees."

"What!" Mark nearly fell out of the tree as he started scrambling down the trunk.

Then he heard a screen door slam.

Mark peeked through the leaves. An old man was working his way down the front porch steps, yelling, "Aha! Caught you!"

Mark looked at the ground and considered his chances of getting down before the old man reached the tree. Then he saw the long barrel of a shotgun.

Patti shrieked, screaming at Mark, "Hurry!"

She stepped back, stumbled and then took off running. Mark reached the lowest branch and swung his legs down to jump. It was as far as he got. He was helplessly hanging on the branch when the old man rounded the tree.

"I've warned you kids!" he shouted, aiming the shotgun at Mark's rear end.

Mark closed his eyes, his heart pounding wild rhythms in his chest.

"Don't," he squeaked.

Just then, the old man pulled the trigger.

CHAPTER FIVE

Tom Riley's Alarm

Mark listened for the tell-tale roar, and tensed, fearing the sting of shotgun pellets. Instead he heard a gentle spraying sound, as warm water soaked through his clothes. He opened his eyes and looked down at the wet seat of his pants.

"I got you fair and square!" Tom Riley shouted, laughing as he pulled the trigger on his water-squirting shotgun.

Then he turned and called, "You can come out from behind that tree, Patti Eldridge. I got your friend!"

Patti stumbled out of her hiding place doubled over with laughter.

Mark dropped from the tree with a squish. He brushed at the water on the back of his pants while Patti continued laughing helplessly. Tom did, too.

Everyone in this town is crazy, Mark thought.

"It's a game," Patti finally said. "If Mr. Riley finds any-one climbing his apple tree, he gives them a shot from his water gun."

"Thanks for telling me." Mark frowned, tugging at his soaked pants.

Tom put out his hand for Mark to shake. "We haven't been properly introduced. I'm Tom Riley."

"I'm Mark. Mark Prescott." As they shook hands, Mark felt the callouses on Mr. Riley's palm.

"Mark is living in Mrs. Schaeffer's house," Patti explained. "She was his grandma."

"I see," Tom said and hitched his thumbs into his over-alls. "Your grandma was a good woman. Now tell me what you're doing out here besides picking my apples and getting a shower."

"Mr. Whittaker sent us," Patti blurted out.

"He sent me," Mark amended. "I'm his new employee."

"Oh," Tom said, "then you must be here for the part to the Imagination Station."

"Yeah, both of us!" Patti added.

"Then you'd better come with me."

They walked to the house while Tom explained how he helped Whit with some of the inventions and kept the extra parts on his workroom bench. Mark imagined the two men working under a dim light as they discussed and created and invented all sorts of magical things. The thought held wonder for Mark, and he looked at Tom Riley with different eyes.

The summer heat hadn't pierced the walls of the Riley home. It was cool down in the basement and back where the workroom was located. The workbench had a large assortment of tools and gadgets. Some of them Mark recognized, others he didn't.

Tom glanced around with confusion.

"The part for the Imagination Station," Mark reminded him.

"That's right," Tom chuckled, patting Mark on the shoulder. Then he reached to an upper shelf and brought down a mysterious object wrapped in white cloth. "This is what you came for," he said, carefully setting the component on the bench.

Mark stepped closer as Tom pulled the cloth aside. The thing looked like a black grapefruit with all sorts of transistors and computer parts attached to it. Tom gently placed it in a box and cushioned it with rags.

"What does it do?" Patti asked.

Tom stuffed more rags into the box. "It's a power unit. It's one of four in the Imagination Station. Together they make it work. Whit said one blew out when he tried it this morning."

"It must be pretty powerful to make such a big noise,"

Patti said.

"Mostly noise and smoke," Tom replied. "We built it so it wouldn't blow up if anything went wrong. That's one reason it's so heavy."

"Still scary," Patti said quietly.

Tom nodded. "I reckon it is, if you don't know what to expect."

As if struck by a new thought, Tom reached up and grabbed another gadget from the shelf. "Oh, tell Whit I finished the alarm. He knows how to hook it up."

Mark looked closely at this new piece. It resembled a clock.

"Next time the Imagination Station has a mind to blow up, this alarm will warn Whit before it happens." Tom patted the alarm proudly.

"It even has a test button," he added, pushing a small red circle on the top. The alarm started to tick.

Mark took a step back.

Tom continued, "You push this button, and in thirty seconds the alarm will go off. That gives you time to prepare for it. It's a little loud."

They watched intently for the remaining fifteen seconds or so. Even though they knew the time was up, the bell blasted so loud it startled them all when it finally went off.

"Wow!" Mark exclaimed.

Tom laughed. "If that doesn't warn Whit something's

wrong, nothing will." Tom put a lid on the box and handed it to Mark. "Be careful, son. I only have a couple more of these left."

"I'll be very careful," Mark promised.

Tom led the way back upstairs for homemade lemonade. Afterward, he walked them toward the woods, chatting cheerfully about Whit and Odyssey and expressing his hope that they would come to visit again sometime. Patti said they would. As they said goodbye, Tom gave Mark an apple, which he put inside the box.

Mark remembered his promise to be careful and clutched the box so tightly his arms began to ache. He could have asked Patti to carry it awhile, but he was too proud.

Once again they took Patti's shortcut through the woods. This time Patti asked Mark questions about himself. It was awkward at first. He didn't like to talk about himself, but she persisted. Finally he told her why they had to move to Odyssey, being careful not to mention that all the trouble was his fault. He didn't tell her his plans for the Imagination Station, either.

"That's sad," Patti said about Mark's parents. He thought she meant it.

"I wrote my dad a letter," he added brightly.

"Is that the one we took to the post office?" Patti asked.

Mark nodded and said, "I asked him to come visit for the Fourth of July."

Mark felt funny telling her. He hadn't told anyone—not even his mom—what was in the letter.

Patti's face lit up. "Do you think he will?"

"Yeah! He said on the phone if I ever wanted anything to write and ask, so I did. It's a long weekend. He has to come."

"How long before he answers it?" Patti asked.

"He'll probably call when..." Mark stopped, suddenly remembering. The letter was still stuffed in his back pocket. With all the excitement over the Imagination Station, he had forgotten all about it. His heart sank.

Patti searched Mark's face. "What's wrong?"

"I was going to mail the letter today." Mark's voice was low again.

How could he have been so forgetful? He had a mission.

He quickened his step. He had to get the box to Mr. Whittaker, find a clean envelope and mail the letter. They came out of the woods on Glossman Street, the road leading to the center of town. They had followed it only a short way when they heard the rattle of bikes behind them. By the time they turned to see who it was, they were surrounded.

Mark groaned quietly.

Joe Devlin and five of his friends climbed off their bikes. "Hello, Patti." Joe smiled viciously. "Guess it's time to finish the fight we had this morning."

CHAPTER SIX

A Narrow Escape

I'm not afraid of you, Joe," Patti said with a sneer. "I beat you this morning; I can beat you again."

"Quiet, Patti," Mark whispered.

"You sneaked up on me this morning, that's all," Joe said, angrily. "Let's see how you do in a fair fight."

"My dad said boys shouldn't hit girls," Mark offered feebly.

"My dad says the same thing," Joe mocked, "but Patti isn't a girl. Are you, Patti? You dress like a boy, and you act like a boy. I guess you think you can fight like a boy, too, huh?" Joe stepped closer, and so did his gang.

"You want to fight? Then let's fight," Patti challenged, positioning herself for the attack. "And Mark won't rescue you this time, either!"

"He won't have to rescue me. He'll have to rescue you like boyfriends are supposed to." Joe laughed. His friends joined in, taunting and cackling.

"He's not my boyfriend," Patti countered with a blush.

Joe and his boys laughed louder. "Patti's got a boyfriend. Patti's got a boyfriend," they chanted.

"You guys are idiots!" Patti shouted. "Come on, Joe, you think you're so tough. I'll show you how tough you are!" Her face turned red.

She thinks she's going to fight them all! Mark thought.

Joe crouched slightly, as if he were going to jump at Patti.

Mark tensed and did the only thing he could think to do. "Wait!" he yelled.

All eyes turned to Mark.

"We can't get in a fight. We might break what's in this box," Mark announced.

"What do I care what's in your box?" Joe snorted.

"It's not my box," Mark explained. "It's Mr. Whittaker's box. And there's no telling what might happen if it gets broken."

Joe squinted, looking at the box. "That's Mr. Whittaker's? My dad says he's a crazy old man."

A wave of laughter went through the gang.

"Maybe he is," Mark said. "That's why we have to get this box back to him."

Joe shrugged it off. "Mr. Whittaker can't do anything to us," he countered. "Come on, Patti, your boyfriend's stalling."

Patti looked at Mark with a puzzled expression on her face.

"You remember the explosion at Whit's End earlier?" Mark asked.

Joe eyed Mark suspiciously. "Yeah? What about it?"

"I heard it blew up the whole bottom floor!" said one of Joe's gang.

Mark attempted a scowl. "Yeah, well what's in this box caused it. It could happen again if I want. You guys should get out of here before you get blown up. I'm through messing around with you small-town hoods."

"Yeah, sure," Joe said in disbelief. "Nobody's going to get blown up."

"Okay, you asked for it," Mark said and put down the box. "I'll show you!"

Maybe it was curiosity or maybe it was fear, but everyone stood still and watched carefully. Mark took the lid off the box like a magician who was about to pull a rabbit out of a hat. Everyone stepped back.

"I'm telling you, you better get far away from here. You don't know me. I might be crazier than Mr. Whittaker," Mark warned.

Joe and his gang exchanged uneasy looks.

"What are you doing?" Patti asked, moving closer to

Mark.

"Quiet," Mark whispered. Then he said aloud, "You guys have thirty seconds to get away."

Patti glanced at the box and realized what he was up to. Her eyes smiled at him.

Suddenly she shouted, "No! Don't do it!"

Mark punched the red test button on the top of Tom Riley's alarm. It ticked loudly.

Patti bolted away. "I'm getting out of here."

"See you guys later," Mark said, running a short distance away.

Joe's gang looked at the box, and then Joe, and then back at the box. They got tangled up with their bikes as they dragged them off to a safe distance.

Not Joe—he leaned forward to get a better glimpse of the contents.

Mark yelled, "Twenty seconds!"

Startled, Joe jumped and backed up a little.

"Joe," one of his friends called out, "get away from there."

Joe's confidence decreased with each tick.

"Fifteen seconds!" Mark shouted.

Joe moved toward his bike one slow step at a time, never taking his eyes off the box.

His entire gang screamed, "Run!" "Come on, Joe." "Get out of there!"

"Ten seconds!" Mark and Patti called together.

"Nine," Mark continued.

Joe grabbed his bike.

"Eight!"

Joe stumbled as his bike slipped from his hands. He got up and moved quickly away from the box.

"Seven!"

The gang moved farther away, tripping over one another as they did.

"Six!"

Joe's walk turned to a jog.

"Five!"

"Hit the dirt!" Patti screamed.

"Four!"

Several of the boys crouched near the ground.

"Three!"

Joe started to run.

"Two!"

Joe fell to the ground with the rest of his gang.

"One!"

They all watched expectantly.

Nothing happened.

Patti looked at Mark with concern.

Mark shrugged. "The timing must be off."

Joe and his gang growled and slowly stood. Joe started to issue a new threat.

But the alarm went off with such a shrill blast that Joe and his company dropped to the ground again.

"Into the woods!" Mark exclaimed, rushing for the box. Without breaking his stride, Mark grabbed the box and took off running.

Joe shouted, his anger growing with each word, "We've been conned! Get 'em!"

Patti ran through the woods. Mark was close behind, struggling not to drop the box. His heart pounded furiously. He dodged piles of leaves and broken branches. The shouts and curses of Joe and his friends followed them.

"This way," Patti gasped, moving off the path into a deeper part of the woods.

She ducked behind a tree and gestured for Mark to do the same. He tripped, knocking them both into a cushion of leaves. They lay still and struggled to quiet their hard breathing. Mark heard thumping sounds of running feet. Threats and curses were swallowed by labored panting as Joe's gang ran down the path, passed by and then faded away.

Mark relaxed and sighed with relief.

Patti began to laugh softly. "I've never seen them so scared," she said between giggles.

Mark smiled.

"Great idea about the box," she said, laughing harder. "I wish I'd thought of that."

"You were too busy trying to get yourself killed," Mark stated with a hint of sarcasm.

He closed his eyes, enjoying the soft bed of leaves. For the moment he was so tired that he didn't care about the letter to his father or the Imagination Station or any of the problems that weighed on his mind. He smiled, feeling relieved they had escaped.

"Oh!" Patti's startled gasp jolted him back to reality.

Then she shouted, "Watch out!"

A group of strangely dressed boys stood over Mark, their spears and arrows pointing directly at his chest.

CHAPTER SEVEN

Captured!

Have we gone back in time? Mark wondered. His captors were carrying homemade shields, spears, bows and arrows. They also had on tunics that made them look like they had stepped out of an old Bible movie. *But are these characters real?* he wondered.

Patti quickly ended the notion. "I know who you are," she said. "I recognize you behind that disguise, George Baldwin. You, too, Billy MacPherson."

"We do not know these strange names," one of them said.

Another one stepped forward. "I am Jonathan. Are you Amalekites or are you with the forces of King Saul?"

"Quit playing around. You know who I am, Pete."

Patti's tone was mocking. She started to get up, but the spears and arrows persuaded her otherwise.

"Cut it out!" she said.

"Well?" the one called Jonathan asked more forcefully.

Mark thought back to the Old Testament stories, remembering how David was best friends with Jonathan, son of Saul. But Saul, king of Israel, had chased the boy David. King Saul was jealous because God had chosen David to be the next king. Saul had also fought the Amalekites, the enemies of Israel.

Mark decided to play along with this Jonathan's game. "We are not Amalekites. And we are not servants of the King," Mark said, trying to sound official, "except as loyal subjects."

"Oh, brother." Patti rolled her eyes in disbelief.

"Why are you in our woods?" Jonathan asked. "We are true Israelites and do not look kindly to foreigners in our lands."

"We're trying to get this box back to Mr. Whittaker. But Joe and his gang tried to stop us." Then Patti said with anger, "Get those sticks out of my face!"

Jonathan gestured for them both to rise. "Come with us," he said.

Mark obeyed, clutching the box tightly. He considered trying the alarm trick again but decided that this gang wouldn't fall for it.

"Where are we going?" Patti asked.

"You'll see," Jonathan answered.

As they walked through the woods, Mark hoped Patti knew where they were because he was lost. He also hoped this band of "Israelites" wouldn't hurt them, but he couldn't be sure.

Suddenly Jonathan signaled for them to stop. "Blindfolds," he said.

"Oh, no you don't," Patti said, stepping away from them. A couple of Iraelites grabbed her.

"Hey, let go!" she yelled, straining against them.

"You won't get hurt,"the leader said. "This is so you won't see the entrance to the hideout."

Patti continued to argue and struggle as they blindfolded her.

Mark thought it was a little too dramatic but decided not to fight them. He wanted to get this over with, since the box was painfully heavy in his arms.

Then the Israelites spun Mark and Patti around several times to make sure they couldn't track where they were being taken.

As they quietly marched through the woods, Mark listened carefully. Natural noises seemed amplified—the padding of their feet on the leaves, birds singing, a distant voice of a mother calling her child. And the smells were familiar—a dark woodsy odor, green pine and damp leaves.

Eventually the sounds and smells gave way to something new: fresh air and distant traffic. They were near an opening to the woods. But Mark had no way of guessing where they might be.

Then they stopped again.

"Here," a voice said.

Mark shifted the box's weight from one arm to the other. He heard brushing noises, as if someone were sweeping a wooden floor. Then it sounded, as if a latch were being lifted on a large door. A creak and a groan followed when the door—if it was a door—opened.

"Watch the steps," someone else said.

"How can I watch the steps with this stupid blindfold on?" Patti asked. Her voice sounded distant when she spoke.

Mark was led forward and then down a stairway. Outside noises were swallowed up by a hollow nothingness. Their footsteps squeaked and clicked as they walked. Mark thought they might be in an underground tunnel. A door closed behind them with a heavy iron clang.

We're in a dungeon, Mark imagined. *A cobwebbed castle with shackles and chains, musty smells, mildewed walls and instruments of torture.* The thought didn't faze him. By now, his arms ached from carrying the box. He could endure anything, if only they would let him set it down.

They stopped again, and another door opened. They were led into another place where the air was fresher, the mustiness gone. But it was still very quiet.

"Sit down," a voice ordered. "You can put the box by your feet."

Mark gladly obliged, reaching back to make sure there was a place to sit. He felt the rugged texture of a wooden bench and sat on it. Patti sat next to him.

"Can we take these blindfolds off now?" Patti asked. "This whole thing is really dumb."

"In a minute," came the reply.

Mark and Patti sat patiently. Mark wondered what was supposed to happen next. All was quiet.

Too quiet, Mark thought.

"Hello?" he called.

No answer.

"Anybody here?" he asked.

No answer again.

He reached up and slowly pushed up his blindfold. It took a moment for his eyes to adjust. He blinked a few times. The room was obviously some sort of basement, but the Israelites had slipped away.

"They're gone," Mark whispered to Patti.

They both took off their blindfolds.

Mark blinked again. The room came into focus. It was obviously a workroom cluttered with tools, gadgets and strange parts. A large machine sat in the center of the floor.

"Where are we?" Patti asked. "Look at this place!"

"I don't know," Mark replied. He couldn't take his eyes

off the machine. Inside it, lights twinkled like a Christmas tree through the deep-brown colored glass.

"What is that thing?" Patti asked, mouth hanging open with awe.

A low, resonant voice answered, "It's the Imagination Station."

CHAPTER EIGHT

The Imagination Station

John Avery Whittaker stood at the door, a broad smile on his face. "Do you like it?"

Mark's eyes locked on the machine, as he walked slowly toward it. *So this is the Imagination Station! This is how to get things back to the way they used to be.* Mark circled it, taking in every detail.

"You brought the part," Whit said, stooping to retrieve the box from the floor. "Thank you."

"Hey, Whit," Patti began, "what's with those kids who brought us here? The . . . what do you call them?"

"The Israelites," Whit said. "You took so long getting back with the part, I decided to send them out to look for you."

"Yeah, but the Israelites? I never heard of a gang called the Israelites," Patti said.

"It's make-believe," Whit answered, pulling the contents from Tom Riley's box. "They pretend they're a band of King David's men. Sometimes they battle the forces of wicked King Saul; other times they're off fighting the Amalekites. It's fun, and they get to learn the Bible in the process."

"Oh," Patti remarked with an easy acceptance.

Whit turned to Mark. "What do you think of my little invention?"

The question startled Mark. He was deep in thought about the machine and didn't realize Whit was standing next to him. "It looks great," Mark replied. "Does it work?"

"Not yet. I hope it will after I put this power source in and make a few more adjustments."

Whit flipped a panel switch on the side of the Imagination Station, and the station went dark. Then he began to unscrew bolts that held a small metal plate attached to the back of the machine.

Mark watched carefully. "Can I help?" he finally asked.

Whit handed the metal plate to Mark. "You can hold this while I get the new part hooked up."

Mark held the plate while Whit went to work. He undid a bolt here, attached a wire there, fastened a clip to this side, adjusted a screw to that side. He moved quickly, with the confidence of a man who knew exactly what he was doing.

"It's kind of cute," Patti observed.

Mark groaned inwardly. *A machine this powerful isn't cute,* he thought. He wished she would go home.

"We're almost there," Whit said softly as he continued working.

Mark's mind wandered. He pictured himself climbing into the machine, pushing the buttons and riding back in time to the day his dad left. It was real. He could do it!

"Mark?" Whit's eyebrow was cocked. His arms were outstretched for the metal plate Mark was holding.

"Sorry," Mark mumbled as he handed it over.

"Daydreaming?" Whit asked, bolting the plate back to the machine.

Mark shuffled. "Yeah, I guess."

"About what?"

Mark looked at Whit and wondered how much he should say. Finally he shrugged. "I was imagining what it would be like to go back in time."

"Ah, that depends on where you want to go," Whit said.

Patti jumped into the conversation, "I want to go back to . . . to . . ." She screwed up her face, realizing she had started to speak without knowing what she wanted to say. "I could go anywhere," she concluded.

"It also depends on why you want to go," Whit added.

Mark looked deeply into Whit's face. Did this kind old man know more about people and what they were thinking than he ever let on?

"What do you mean, why? Why not? I think it would be fun," Patti said.

"Fun, yes. A way to learn, too. But sometimes people want to go back in time for other reasons." Whit turned to his workbench and fiddled with one of the gadgets.

Mark felt uneasy. He had a strange feeling Whit was referring to him.

"Why would you want to go back in time, Mark?" Whit asked casually.

Mark swallowed and said, "I . . . I thought I'd like to go back to . . . to see my dad. That's all."

Whit turned slightly and asked, "Go back to see your dad? Why can't you see him now?"

"It's not the same now," Mark answered. "Everything's different. He's different."

Mark's heart pounded, and his voice shook. He didn't want to talk about this. Not to Whit. Not to anybody. He just wanted to get in the Imagination Station and go back.

"I don't know that going back in time will help," Whit said quietly. "Unless you think you're going back to change things."

Whit now faced Mark full on. His eyes seemed to search Mark's. But Mark couldn't speak.

Whit spoke firmly. "Changing the past will never really

bring present happiness, you know."

Their gazes locked. The statement hung between them on an invisible string.

No, you're wrong! Mark wanted to scream. *It has to make us happy again. Don't you see? It's all my fault my parents broke up. If I could go back, I could change it. I will change it!*

But Mark didn't say any of those things. He stared at his shoes instead.

Whit sighed deeply. "The Imagination Station isn't ready for operation anyway, not until I make those adjustments. I guess it doesn't make a whole lot of difference. Let's go on upstairs and forget about it."

"Yeah, let's go," Patti agreed.

CHAPTER NINE

Bad News

Mark spent the rest of the day doing errands around Whit's End. Patti stayed on even though she wasn't needed anymore, but she didn't seem to care. At dinnertime, they went their separate ways.

On his way home, Mark plotted how he could get to the Imagination Station. Whit was wrong, Mark felt. He could go back in time and change things. He had to.

At home, while he and his mom were eating dinner, she asked him about his day. Then she talked about all the nice people she had met shopping that afternoon and the ones who knew Mark's grandmother. Mark's mind drifted away.

He helped his mom clean up the dishes, and then

excused himself to go to his bedroom. He turned on the light, sat at the small rolltop desk and carefully opened the crumpled letter he had written to his father. Had it only been this morning that he had met Patti and ruined the letter when he pulled her off Joe? The time between then and now seemed longer than any one day should be.

Mark double-checked the letter spread out before him. His handwriting was as neat as he could make it; he wanted everything to be perfect.

> *Dear Dad,*
>
> *Hi. It's me, Mark. How are you? I'm fine. I don't like Odyssey very much, even though I haven't seen all of it yet. But I know I won't like it because you aren't here. Will you come to visit? You said if I asked you to come, you would. Please come for the Fourth of July weekend. We can do fireworks like we always used to.*
>
> *Dad, I figured out that it was my fault you went away. I'm sorry. If you come back, I promise to clean my room and put my clothes away and not leave my sneakers in the middle of the living room floor for you to trip over when you come home. I'll do anything you want me to, if you come back.*
>
> *But come for the Fourth of July anyway.*
>
> *Love,*
>
> *Mark*
>
> *PS I really mean it.*

Mark carefully wrote out his father's name and address on a clean envelope. His mom had given it to him earlier, along with a curious look. Mark wondered how she would respond if she knew what he had written.

The phone rang, making him jump enough to mess up the zip code. "Oh, no," he moaned.

Now he would have to get another clean envelope from his mother. He tossed the pen on the desk and frowned. "I can't even write a stupid zip code," he said to himself.

Downstairs, he heard his mother in the kitchen on the phone.

It's probably one of the women she met shopping today, he figured.

He walked quickly through the dining room, slowing only when he heard his mom's tone of voice.

"No!" she said in a harsh whisper. "You will not put that responsibility on me. If you want him to know, tell him yourself."

Mark heard the squeaking of her rubber soles as she paced across the kitchen floor.

He stood near the doorway and listened.

"It's one thing for you to take the coward's way out with me. It's another thing to do it with him. He deserves better. You hold on, and I'll get him." His mother paused. "Yes, now, Richard."

She put the phone down as Mark moved away from the doorway. He tried to act as if he had just walked into the room.

"Mark!" his mother called. Then spotting him in the dining room, she said, "Oh, there you are."

"Hi," Mark replied nervously. "I was looking for a new envelope."

She moved close to him and touched him lightly on the shoulder. Her voice was like a soft blanket, so different from the one he had heard her use on the phone.

"Your . . . your father is on the phone," she said. "He wants to talk to you."

Mark's heart raced. *This isn't good news,* he thought as he walked to the kitchen phone. *Something's wrong.*

He looked for some assurance from his mother. She was gone. It was just like the morning his dad left, when Mark had stood outside on the steps of his house in Washington, D.C., and looked back at the front door. He had wanted to see his mother's smile. Something that said it would be all right. But she had closed the door. Only this time, he heard her feet padding up the stairs. Was it his imagination, or did he hear a sob?

When Mark picked up the receiver, the phone line seemed to hiss like a charmed snake. "Hello?"

"Hello, son," Richard Prescott said cheerfully. "How are you?"

"I'm okay, Dad," Mark answered. "I'm mailing you a letter. I was going to mail it today, but it got scrunched up in my back pocket when I—"

"Mark," his dad interrupted, his voice sounding tight. "I want to hear about the letter. But I have to tell you something. Okay?"

Mark felt his cheeks flush. "Yeah, okay."

The pause seemed endless.

Then his father said, "Son . . . "

Mark held his breath.

"Son, I've been doing a lot of thinking. And, well, your mother and I have been talking about it." The line crackled.

Whatever his father was about to say, Mark knew he didn't want to hear it. "Dad, listen, you got to come for the Fourth of July weekend, okay? I want you to see Odyssey and Grandma's house and my bedroom. I keep my bedroom really clean, Dad. You'll be proud. I don't even leave my shoes in the middle of the floor. So you have to come and— "

"Mark," his dad interjected, "my separation from your mother was a way to see if… if we could work it out or… or make it more permanent."

"Dad, listen—"

"No, Mark, you have to understand what I'm saying. I can't come for the Fourth of July." His father's voice sounded strained, full of tears. "See, your mother and I are going to proceed with the divorce. We won't . . . can't live together anymore."

Mark felt cold and heartsick. His father continued talking as Mark gently put down the receiver. Mark didn't want to know what he was saying. He didn't care. He only knew that his father wasn't coming for the Fourth of July. His father wasn't coming for anything ever again.

The thought was enormous, larger than anything Mark had ever tried to fit into his brain. It was so big, in fact, that scalding tears slid down his cheeks.

Mark walked to the front door and stepped out into the warm summer night. He knew what he had to do.

CHAPTER TEN

A Close Call

Mark wiped the tears from his face and looked across the street. Whit's End looked like a dark giant that was fast asleep. Mark glanced around for oncoming cars and then stepped from the curb.

He should have been afraid of what he planned to do. He wasn't. His fear was numbed by the news from his father.

Mark examined his watch in the dim street light. It was 9:38 P.M. Whit's End had closed at nine. Would Whit lock the front door of his shop in such a small, trustworthy town?

Probably, Mark guessed. *No town is that trustworthy.*

He silently made his way around to the side of the large

building. He crept along like a shadow on the wall, searching for a way to get inside.

The basement has a window, he recalled. *Maybe it's unlocked.*

He ran toward it and then slowed down, approaching cautiously.

Whit might be working late, he thought.

He carefully peered in the window. A small light, near the workbench, sent a colorful pool of warmth throughout the basement. No one was around. All was silent and still. The Imagination Station sat waiting.

Mark's heart quickened. He pushed on the window frame, but it didn't budge. He knelt, searched for the latch, finally spotting it near the top of the sill. It was in the locked position. Mark stood and leaned against the wall. He didn't know what to do.

"Hey! What are you doing?" someone shouted.

Mark jumped up and looked around to see who it was. Beneath the pale street light, he saw a police car. A large policeman stood nearby.

"Don't move!" the officer said, turning on the squad car spotlight and adjusting it toward Whit's End.

Everything in Mark's being told him to run as fast as he could, so he did.

"Hey!" the policeman shouted. "Come back here!"

Mark wasn't sure where he was going in the darkness. He thought he remembered a grove of trees somewhere behind Whit's End and a wide-open park beyond them.

"Stop!" the policeman yelled, taking up the chase.

Mark wondered if Odyssey policemen shot at their suspects.

The grove of trees appeared in the summer moonlight. Mark dove into the shadows, tripping over logs and leaves, feeling the sting of an odd branch lashing at his face.

The policeman was closing in.

Mark scrambled behind a fallen oak. A large root caught his foot and sent him sailing through the air. He landed in a pile of leaves. The fall knocked the wind out of him. He couldn't moan. He couldn't speak. He couldn't breathe. In fact he couldn't do anything but lie there gasping, trying to take in some air.

The officer stopped at the edge of the woods and turned his flashlight on. The beam bounced off the trees, scanning in all directions. For a moment the light rested near Mark; then it moved away again.

"Come on, kid. I know you're in here somewhere," the policeman called out.

Do Odyssey policemen throw boys in jail? Mark wondered. *If they do, is it for the rest of their lives?*

He imagined his arrest. They would take his picture and make him hold one of those little cards with a number on it. His mother would be ashamed. His father would refuse to speak to him. The newspapers would say he was another product of a broken home. And Whit would never ever let him near the Imagination Station again.

Mark prepared himself for the worst.

But the policeman didn't come into the woods. He let the flashlight beam do the searching for him. It spotted trees and leaves and a fat old owl that hooted and flew away. Finally muttering something Mark couldn't hear, the policeman turned and walked back toward Whit's End. The night was quiet again except for the ongoing sound of crickets.

Mark sat up. What was he going to do now? If he went back to Whit's End, the police might be waiting. And if he went home, he would have to wait for another time to get to the Imagination Station. But would there ever be another time?

Mark's feelings told him there wouldn't be. What he had to do, he had to do this very minute.

When he started to push himself up off the ground, his hands slipped, and he felt something cold and hard. He jerked up and slid away from the spot.

When he felt convinced that the thing wouldn't hurt him, Mark crawled closer to see if he could make out what it was. He reached down to touch it again. It was metallic like the side of a car. He felt rivets along a straight edge.

What is this thing? he questioned as he scurried around it.

He brushed the leaves away with his hand, wishing he

had a broom. A broom! Then he remembered the brushing sound he had heard when the Israelites led him and Patti back to Whit's End. They had brushed the leaves away and opened a door. A door to Whit's End!

As he was clearing off the leaves and dirt, his hand banged against a latch. Mark smiled with satisfaction. It was the way in!

Mark looked around to make sure the policeman was gone. He didn't want to risk getting caught now. All remained quiet.

Sweat mingled with the dirt on his hands as Mark grabbed the handle. The latch groaned and clicked but didn't release the door.

Mark adjusted his stance, planting his feet firmly on the ground. Then he yanked up on the latch until the door gave way. It wasn't as heavy as it looked. The hinges creaked in protest as Mark swung the door over and gently placed it on the ground. Pleased with himself, he looked down at a large black square hole.

Now what should he do? Mark's brain clicked over the details. What else had he heard when the Israelites led him this way? They went down a few stairs and then followed a long tunnel. Stairs and a tunnel.

Mark looked across the yard to Whit's End. It seemed like a distant fortress now. Even so, the tunnel must go underground from this point all the way to Whit's End— in complete darkness. Mark gulped hard.

Did Odyssey have rats? Large spiders? Snakes? Mark felt a chill trickle down his spine, wondering what might be waiting for him in the black hole.

Taking a deep breath, he tried to decide if the journey was worth it. He thought of his mother and father, his home in Washington, D.C., his happiness.

Mark wished the large black hole would give some hint of friendship. It didn't. He braced himself and stepped into it anyway.

He made it to the bottom step before he expected to and nearly fell. Reaching out to steady himself, he felt the walls, which were rough and cool. His eyes started to adjust to the darkness, but he saw only more darkness. He moved forward slowly.

He began to sing tuneless "la, la's" and "da, da's." It was something he had learned to do to help fight the fear, to keep monsters away in the closet. He couldn't remember where he had learned the rule, but it had always proven true: Make music, and you'll feel safe.

Mark didn't really believe in monsters, though. But he sang anyway. No sense taking any chances.

A sudden thought stopped him. *Do rats and spiders and snakes understand the rule?* He hoped so.

Mark wasn't sure where he was now. Somewhere under the backyard of Whit's End, of course, but where? How far did he have to go? He thought he heard a noise behind him.

Is someone else in the passageway? Maybe Whit has someone or something down here to keep guard.

Mark's stomach tangled up into a hundred knots. He wanted to get out of this hole. He wanted to scream. He wanted the policeman to come and save him.

He gasped, thinking he heard a low pounding nearby. Or was it his heart? Maybe he should turn back. Maybe he was crazy to do this in the first place.

He looked behind him. The small amount of light that had spilled into the doorway was gone. Up ahead, Mark could see a tiny dot of yellow. He prayed it was the door into Whit's End.

Something brushed against his leg. A scream caught in his throat, unable to come out. He pressed hard against the wall, and whatever it was brushed against his leg again. Mark kicked out wildly, but his foot didn't strike anything. He felt frozen with fear and stood as still as he could.

Then came a sound like a violin string being scratched. "Meow!"

Mark gave a startled jump. "A cat! A stupid cat!" he muttered to himself.

It meowed again and started its purring motor. The creature, unaware of Mark's terror, rubbed against his leg once more. Mark relaxed. He wasn't sure if he loved the cat for not being a monster or hated it for scaring him so badly.

When Mark's rubbery legs decided they could move again, he continued moving forward. The cat went ahead of him in the darkness, meowing, as if it were guiding him along. Mark willingly followed; he was less afraid now. Having the cat nearby made it all right.

The tiny yellow glow grew larger as he got closer. It was a night-light outside a door. Mark assumed it was the door leading into the basement of Whit's End. He sighed with relief.

The cat brushed against his leg and meowed again. *Poor cat,* Mark thought. *It must have gotten locked in the tunnel somehow.*

Locked! Mark groaned. *What if the door is locked?*

Mark hadn't even thought of that possibility. It seemed logical to him that if the secret door to the tunnel was unlocked, the secret door to Whit's End would be unlocked, too. Right? Surely he hadn't come all this way to get stopped by a locked door.

Mark reached out and seized the door handle, turning it quickly. The door opened silently on greased hinges. Mark's eyes widened as the room came into focus. It was exactly as they had left it that afternoon. He stared at the cluttered workbench, the orange glow and the Imagination Station.

Mark made sure no one was lurking about when he stepped into the room. His throat was painfully dry, and his breathing was heavy. He circled the machine that remained at the center of his hopes, reaching the panel where Whit had turned off the Imagination Station. Mark looked around once more to make sure he was alone and then reached up and flipped on the silver switch.

At first he wasn't sure it was working. Nothing happened. Then he heard a low hum. Through the smoky glass, he could see the lights on the control panel blinking happily. When Mark opened the door, it made a whooshing sound. He smiled nervously and climbed inside the Imagination Station. It was like climbing into his dad's sports car, small and comfortable.

Fortunately Whit had clearly marked the buttons and switches on the control panel. There was also a small, square message panel in green letters, suggesting that he close the door.

Mark's fingers trembled as he pushed the labeled button. The door shut with another whoosh, followed by a gentle bump.

The message panel displayed the question: *When?* It also indicated a series of numbers beside another label marked: *Day, Date* and *Time of Day.*

Mark turned the knob and twisted the stem of a small clock to provide the information. He thought it was easy. It was so easy, in fact, he was afraid that he might be doing something wrong.

Now the panel displayed the question: *Address, City, Country?* A small keyboard lit up. Mark guessed he was supposed to spell everything out. Since Mark didn't know how to type, he carefully pushed the letters in order. He gave the machine his home address in Washington, D.C., and finished with U.S.A.

"There," he said to himself proudly.

Next, the panel said: *Push the Red Button to Proceed.*

Mark reached for the red button. It blinked invitingly. Then he paused.

This is the right thing to do, he assured himself. He had to get his parents back together. He had to prove to his dad that he could be the son he should be. He had to go back to that day and make everything better, to make everything the way it was.

Mark pushed the blinking red button.

Instantly, a recording of Whit's soothing voice surrounded him, saying, "Welcome to the Imagination Station."

CHAPTER ELEVEN

The Journey Back

The panel lights and message and even the orange glow outside the tinted-glass window vanished. Mark was in total darkness. He wondered if he had blown a fuse or broken the machine. Then suddenly it got very cold.

"I better get out of here," he said aloud. Reaching forward, he tried to find the button to open the door. But instead of the metal and plastic panel, Mark felt something wooden. It was long and shaped like a pole.

"Something's wrong here," he muttered. He felt around, hoping to find a door handle. When Mark found one, he gave it a tug, and the door slid back easily with a hollow crash.

Bright morning light and crisp, frosty air poured in. Mark blinked several times. He had expected to be taken back to his room in Washington, D.C., but the Imagination Station wasn't as precise as that. It wasn't precise at all.

Outside, he saw a trimmed lawn and the back of a house; on the inside, he noticed a rake, lawn mower and folded patio furniture. As best as Mark could figure, the Imagination Station had put him into an outdoor shed. Even worse than that, it wasn't the Prescotts' shed.

"Mark? Mark Prescott? Is that you?"

Mark cupped a hand over his eyes to block the sunlight; he couldn't see who was calling him.

Mr. Moorhead, the old man who lived across the street from the Prescotts, had a large plastic garbage bag in his hand. He was dressed in a bathrobe and slippers.

"What are you doing in there?" he asked angrily, dropping the bag into the can and moving across the lawn toward Mark.

Mark shuffled out of the shed, speechless.

Mr. Moorhead persisted, "You're trying to play hooky by hiding in my shed? Shame on you!"

"No, sir. See, I was— "

"Don't give me any foolish excuses. What would your parents say if they heard about this?" Mr. Moorhead interrupted.

Mark tried to explain, "I wasn't trying to—"

"I'm very disappointed in you," Mr. Moorhead went

on. "I thought you were above this sort of behavior."

"But I . . . ," Mark sputtered, thinking he should make a run for it.

Before he could, Mr. Moorhead grabbed his arm. "Come on with me. I'm taking you back across the street to let your parents deal with you!" He started across the lawn, pulling Mark alongside of him.

Mark considered this a mixed blessing. On one hand, he would get back to his dad. On the other hand, his dad wouldn't be very happy with him. How would Mark explain it?

"See, Dad, I was in the Imagination Station trying to get back to my bedroom, but it put me in Mr. Moorhead's shed instead."

"Sure, Mark," his dad would say. "Make up another story."

Mr. Moorhead rounded his house and crossed the front lawn with Mark in tow.

"I'm sorry to do this to you, son," Mr. Moorhead explained. "But if parents don't nip this sort of behavior in the bud right away, you'll be out driving fast cars and killing yourself with drugs."

Mark looked across the street at his house. *Home! This is it. I made it!*

The familiarity overwhelmed him. He felt a lump form in his throat and grow into a small softball. He was home again. He wanted to cry, a feeling he hadn't expected.

Mark also didn't expect to see his mother pull out of their driveway in her car.

"Hey, Mrs. Prescott!" Mr. Moorhead shouted.

"Mom!" Mark cried out.

She didn't hear their calls. The windows were up, and her back was to them. The car screeched away to their right, stopped at the corner, turned left and disappeared.

A new panic rose in Mark's mind. What time was it? Had the Imagination Station dropped him off at the wrong time, just like it had dropped him in the wrong place? Maybe his dad had already left!

"Well, what do you know about that?" Mr. Moorhead said, scratching his head.

"What time is it?" Mark asked.

"Time for you to be in school!"

My father might be home, Mark thought. *If I could get to the house, it might not be too late.*

He was about to mention this to Mr. Moorhead when he heard the familiar sound of squealing brakes off to their left. Mr. Moorhead and Mark turned at the same time.

It was Mark's school bus. It had pulled up to the stop sign and was ready to turn onto Mark's street.

Mr. Moorhead smiled pleasantly. "Well, well. Guess it's not too late for you to catch the bus, at least."

He pulled Mark to the edge of the curb and began to wave for the long, yellow vehicle to stop. Mark looked up at the windows filled with the half-awake faces he knew so well.

"No." Mark squirmed. "You don't understand."

"What's the matter, Mark? Do you have a test you don't want to take?" Mr. Moorhead's grip tightened.

"I have to go home, Mr. Moorhead. Please, let me go home," Mark begged.

"Are you sick?"

"No, but— "

"Then you're getting on that bus," Mr. Moorhead said with finality.

And that's exactly what Mark did. The bus driver gave him a disapproving look, pulled the lever to close the doors and put the bus in gear. Mr. Moorhead watched with satisfaction. It was his good deed for the day.

Mark turned to the busload of kids. They giggled and smirked at him.

"What happened to you?" Joe Hirschman asked. "How come you had to get escorted to the bus?"

The other kids giggled.

"Sit down!" the bus driver barked.

Mark walked down the aisle to find a seat. His mind raced. What was he going to do? The bus was taking him to school! He would miss his dad! He peered longingly out the side window as they passed his house. Mark collapsed on a seat next to Kenny Ellis.

"What's the matter with you?" Kenny asked. "You look like you're in some kind of trouble."

Mark didn't like Kenny much; he was considered a troublemaker. But seeing his uncombed hair and the gap in his front teeth made Mark realize that he had missed the boy. Mark was filled with the desire to tell Kenny that he had moved away to a place called Odyssey. He wanted to confess about breaking into Whit's End to get to the Imagination Station.

I came back in time, Mark wanted to say. *My dad is going to leave, and I'm trying to stop him.* But he didn't say any of those things.

Instead, he whispered urgently, "I have to get off this bus."

"Don't we all," Kenny chuckled.

"I have to get home to see my dad. It's an emergency." Mark's eyes filled with tears.

No, I don't want to cry in front of all these kids, he thought. *I can't cry.*

Kenny looked concerned. "Tell the bus driver to let you off."

"He won't let me, you know that. He'll tell me to go to the school office and call my parents." Mark swallowed back the softball still growing in his throat. "Then it'll be too late."

Kenny frowned and said, "It's that important, huh?"

"Yeah," Mark said.

Kenny stared thoughtfully out the window. "All right, you owe me your lunch money." He smiled and then climbed over Mark to get into the bus aisle.

"Huh?"

"I'm going to act like I'm hurt. When the bus driver stops, you ditch out the emergency exit in the back." Kenny pressed his face close to Mark's. "This is an emergency, right?"

"Yeah, but won't the alarm go off?" Mark asked, suddenly afraid of the scene it might cause.

Kenny rolled his eyes impatiently. "Do you want off the bus or not?"

"Yes, I do."

"Then get moving," Kenny said as he dropped onto the aisle floor. He clutched his leg and cried like a dying cow in a hailstorm.

The bus driver looked up into his large rearview mirror. "What's going on?"

"Stop the bus! Something's wrong with Kenny!" yelled Karen Sizer.

CHAPTER TWELVE

An Empty House

When the bus pulled over to stop, Mark yanked the latch on the emergency door, swung it open and jumped out. An alarm honked again and again. The bus driver shouted at Mark, but he kept running without looking back.

I can't be too late, I can't be too late, Mark thought, puffing as he ran. Through side streets and backyards, he pushed himself faster than he had ever gone before.

I'll tell Dad I'm sorry. I'll promise to keep my room clean. I'll keep the television turned down low. I'll stay out of his way when he has work to do. I'll be the perfect son. It's all my fault. All my fault. I'll make it up to him somehow. Somehow.

On and on Mark ran, feeling the morning chill. He was dressed for an Odyssey June, not a cold February in Washington, D.C. But it didn't matter to him. As long as his father was home.

Please, be home, Mark begged silently.

He skidded around the corner of the Taylors' house next door to his own and then suddenly pulled back. Mr. Moorhead was setting his garbage cans out at the end of the driveway.

Does he spend his entire day with trash? Mark wondered.

Mark crouched down, sneaking behind the Taylors' car. He moved behind the bushes lining their front porch and then the tree at the edge of the house. He couldn't go any farther without being seen. He waited and silently prayed for something to draw Mr. Moorhead's attention away.

Nothing happened. Mr. Moorhead continued to fiddle with his garbage cans. Unable to stand the wait anymore, Mark prepared to make a dash for it just as Mrs. Moorhead appeared at the front door. She told Mr. Moorhead he had a telephone call.

When he turned toward his house, Mark seized the moment and sprinted to the porch, his very own porch, and ran up the stairs. Finally! He opened the storm door, slipped in and quickly turned the knob on their large front door. It was locked.

Locked! Mark nearly screamed. *Why did they lock the front door?*

What if he had an emergency at school, like he cut himself or something and had to come home all of a sudden? He couldn't get in! He would have to sit on the front porch and bleed to death.

Suddenly he remembered the key his parents kept under the back doormat for emergencies. He felt silly.

Watching carefully for Mr. Moorhead or any other nosy neighbor, Mark dashed down the porch stairs and scrambled to the rear of the house. He rounded the corner and barely missed colliding with their trash cans, only to rush headlong into a stack of firewood.

"Stupid, stupid, stupid," Mark said to himself as he pushed the logs away and got to his feet.

How could he forget so quickly? He climbed the stairs to the brown rubber doormat and knelt down. Breathless, he tossed the mat aside.

It revealed an exact square of the mat, two dead worms and no key. Mark looked again. One of the worms wasn't dead, but the key was still gone.

"No," Mark moaned.

This can't be happening. Is this a dream or a nightmare? I didn't come all this way to have everything go wrong.

He tried to think of how he could get in. He could pound on the door. He could try all the windows. If his dad was home, he would come running, right?

Mark began to argue with himself. What if his dad was upstairs, out of earshot? What if he was in the shower? What if someone else heard, like Mr. Moorhead, and called the police? What if . . . what if his dad wasn't home?

Had Mark seen the car out front? He couldn't remember. Even if it wasn't parked on the street, sometimes his dad kept it in the garage. What should Mark do? Was it enough of an emergency to justify throwing one of the logs through the back window? Probably not. Then . . . what?

Lost for an answer and tired from all the running, Mark slumped against the door—and fell face first onto the kitchen floor. His arms and legs sprawled out like a spider's on ice. For the first time ever, he noticed the big balls of fuzz under the refrigerator.

He rolled over and sat up. Everything looked so friendly and familiar: the table, pale blue kitchen counters, appliances and the clock radio.

The glowing joy of being home struck him. He pulled himself up to the kitchen table, his eye catching his mother's note placed carefully in the center. It said:

> *Richard,*
> *I don't want to be here when you leave. It hurts too much. I pray to God you know what you're doing.*
> *Julie*

Mark thought, *So that's why Mom left.*

For a moment, Mark tried to imagine his mother's pain, but he couldn't. He knew what he had been feeling but had never bothered to wonder how she felt. In that moment Mark was ashamed of himself.

But only for a moment. What Mark had come back to do still needed to be done. And if he succeeded, his mother wouldn't be hurt at all.

The grandfather clock ticked loudly when Mark passed through the living room to the stairs. The house was clean and so very still. Was this what homes were like when kids were at school? It seemed unnatural to Mark.

He jogged up the stairs, listening intently for any sound, any movement that might let him know his father was home.

A nagging fear whispered in his ear, *You missed him. He's long gone.*

His heart pounded out a drumbeat of growing panic as he headed down the hallway toward his parents' room. On his right, he passed the doorway to his own room. He paused.

His room was exactly as he had left it that morning. The closet was half open with games, toys and scattered clothes threatening to fall out. His bed was carelessly made. His small desk had piles of endless clutter stacked on it, old school papers and gum wrappers. Drawers hung recklessly from his dresser. It was a mess.

No wonder his father had left. No wonder he couldn't stand to live with Mark anymore.

He turned away from the awful disarray and walked more quickly to his parents' room. The door was slightly ajar. Mark peeked in. Everything looked normal. The bed was neatly made, the floor clean, all drawers and doors were closed.

Mark ran to the closet and threw open the door. Hangers were hanging empty and loose. *Richard Prescott no longer lives here,* they announced.

"No!" Mark exclaimed.

But Mark got the same message from the dresser drawers and the medicine cabinet in the bathroom. *Richard Prescott is gone.* The emptiness howled like a Halloween wind. *You missed him. You didn't make it in time. He's gone, gone, gone.*

Mark stood in the middle of the room. The silence screamed at him. For months he had longed for this moment. In the hours since he met Mr. Whittaker, he believed it could really happen. But he hadn't made it in time. It was his one chance to set everything right again, and he had blown it.

Mark sat on the edge of his parents' bed and did the only thing that made sense. He put his face in his hands and began to cry.

CHAPTER THIRTEEN

Mission Accomplished

Mark was lost in his tears when the door downstairs slammed. His ears heard it, his brain made note of it, but Mark couldn't accept the possibility. Then the front storm door slammed again. Mark sprinted to the stairs and took them two at a time to the bottom floor, where he slipped, recovered and then rounded the corner to the front hallway. No one was there.

But someone had been there! The large oak door stood open. Two suitcases sat on the floor next to the storm door. His dad's suitcases! Maybe Mark hadn't missed him.

He was just about to hurry outside when a figure appeared in the window of the storm door. It grew larger as it came up the front steps and then turned into a blur through the frosty glass. The door opened, and the figure stepped inside and reached for the suitcases.

Mark froze in place. He was unable to move or speak. "Dad," Mark finally said, letting out a breath of air.

Richard Prescott turned and stood up straight. He looked surprised. No, he looked shocked. "Mark? What are you doing here? Why aren't you in school?"

Mark remained frozen, silent. The sudden reality of his father standing before him was more than he could take in.

"Son? Are you all right?" Richard Prescott took a step toward Mark, glancing back at his suitcases self-consciously. "Look, you weren't supposed to be here when this happened. I thought you went to school."

Mark's throat was dry when he spoke. "Dad?"

"I was planning on talking to you later, calling or writing. I didn't know how to tell you," his dad said, shoving his hands in the pockets of his winter coat, the coat Mark and his mom had gotten him for Christmas.

"Don't leave, Dad," Mark croaked.

"Mark." His dad's voice was low and full of sadness. He took a couple of steps closer to Mark and knelt.

Mark began to speak slowly at first, and then his words sped up and ran into each other. "I figured it out, Dad. You don't have to leave. I know what's wrong. I know how to make it better. I'll keep my room clean. I'll pick up after myself. I'll leave you alone when you have to work. I'll be good, Dad. You don't have to leave. I know it's all my fault, but I'll make it better. I promise, I will. I'll make it better, please, Dad, I promise."

The words dissolved into tears, and Mark threw himself into his father's arms.

Richard Prescott held his son tightly. His unshaven face pressed against Mark's, scratching it. "Mark . . . Mark listen to me. This isn't your fault. None of it is your fault. Your mother and I . . . "

A gentle hand stroked Mark's hair. His dad continued, "It's my fault. Something's wrong with me. I'm confused. I don't know what's right and wrong anymore, so I'm going away to try to figure it out. It's not your fault. Do you understand?"

Mark sniffled and tried to make sense of it. He wasn't sure he could, but his dad made him want to.

"It's not your room or your messes or . . . or anything about you." His dad began to cry. "There's nothing you can do to change this, Mark. This is something I have to work out. You can't change this."

Mark stepped back from his dad. They looked into each other's red-rimmed, water-filled eyes. Mark believed him.

"I love you," said his dad. "I love you."

When they hugged again, Mark believed that, too. The tears came once more, and Mark buried his face in his father's chest.

"Don't go, Dad. Don't go," he whispered. "Don't

go." His words sounded muffled and strange to his own ears, but Mark kept saying it anyway. "Don't go."

"I'm not going anywhere, Mark."

A different voice now spoke, yet it was full of the same deep love as his father's. Mark pulled away and looked up.

His mother, her cheeks flushed and stained from crying, was looking down at her son.

CHAPTER FOURTEEN

Home Again

Had it been a dream? Had it been some kind of fantasy?

Mark was back in Whit's basement; his mother was holding him in her arms. The Imagination Station hummed quietly only a few feet away. Whit and a policeman were watching the scene quietly.

"Oh, honey," Julie said as she brushed Mark's cheek, "are you all right?"

Mark sighed, "Yeah, I think so."

"I went up to your room to find you and found this instead." She held up the letter Mark had written to his father. "I wish I knew you were feeling these things. We could have talked about it."

Mark shrugged. Why hadn't he talked to his mother? He could have. He should have. Maybe he had thought he knew what she would say. Maybe he had thought she wouldn't understand. As he looked into his mother's face, he knew he was wrong.

"I'm sorry, Mom," he said quietly. That softball was forming in his throat again.

Whit knelt next to them. "I had a feeling that's why you were so interested in the Imagination Station. But, Mark," Whit said, pausing to make sure Mark was listening. "The Imagination Station wasn't created to change the past—only to learn from it."

Mark nodded.

Whit continued warmly, "Things change, Mark. It's as true as the sun rises and falls. And change isn't good or bad, it just is. Sometimes we can control change through the decisions we make, other times we can't. What's important is how we react to change."

Mark glanced at his mother. She smiled gently in agreement.

Whit reached over and rested his hand lightly on Mark's shoulder. "We can try to run away. We can try to change what has already happened, but most of the time it only makes everything worse. The best thing we can do is face up to the changes in our lives and have faith that God is watching over those changes. That's the challenge for all of us."

Mark looked deep into Whit's eyes. They were alive with the meaning of his words.

"I believe," Whit said, "that the greatest adventure is the one I'm having right now. It may not be like yesterday's adventure or even like tomorrow's, but it's the one I'm having now, and that's all that matters." Whit patted Mark's shoulder affectionately and stood.

Then Whit turned to the waiting policeman and said, "I won't be pressing charges, officer. Thank you for all you've done."

"Yes, thank you," Mark's mother said.

"You were very smart to realize the boy you chased into the woods might be the same one Julie reported missing," Whit added.

"Just trying to do my job." The policeman smiled.

"And you've done it well," Whit said.

The officer paused at the door. His voice sounded amazed as he gestured to the Imagination Station. "You mean to say that machine actually works?"

Whit chuckled, pulling the door closed behind them.

Julie searched Mark's face. "Come home, Mark. We have a lot to talk about."

Mark sniffled and nodded.

They hugged long and hard one more time before they left. The Imagination Station hummed happily beside them.

———————

Mark watched the maze of people at the town carnival. It was the Fourth of July weekend, and Odyssey exploded with the celebration. On Main Street an endless parade of floats, bands, baton twirlers and costumed characters passed by. The night sky lit up with the red, white and blues of the fireworks.

Mark sat on a bench near the cotton-candy seller, taking in all the excitement. He could see Whit at the Whit's End Charity Booth. He had invented a variety of games and inventions to raise money for the homeless. Mark had worked on some of them. As part of his punishment for breaking into the Imagination Station, he had to work for Mr. Whittaker for a week without pay. Mark didn't mind. Whit's End was always fun.

Suddenly Mark saw something, someone out of the corner of his eye. He watched closely, a warm rush flowing over him. It was a man who looked a lot like his father. The man turned to kiss his wife while reaching for a little girl's small hand. A soft ache touched Mark's heart.

He turned away and strolled to another part of the carnival. He found his mother trying to hit a bull's-eye with a ball that would knock a clown into a large container of water. Her aim was so poor, the clown finally jumped into the water himself.

His mother laughed hard. Mark thought she seemed happy, even though the two of them had shared a lot of tears since Mark's trip to the past. His dad's leaving wasn't easy for either of them. He understood that now.

She saw Mark and waved. He waved back and then shoved his hands in his pockets and walked on.

Change, he thought. *Like the sun rises and falls, Mr. Whittaker said. Things change. They'll change again.*

Another burst of fireworks added multi-colored stars to the sky, and Mark smiled.

Other books by Paul McCusker
Youth Ministry Comedy & Drama: Better Than Bathrobes but Not Quite Broadway
(co-author Chuck Bolte; Group Books)
Plays
Snapshots & Portraits
(Lillenas Publishing Co.)
Camp W
(Contemporary Drama Service)
Family Outings
(Lillenas Publishing Co.)
The Revised Standard Version of Jack Hill
(Baker's Play Publishing Co.)
Catacombs
(Lillenas Publishing Co.)
The Case of the Frozen Saints
(Baker's Play Publishing Co.)
The Waiting Room
(Baker's Play Publishing Co.)
A Family Christmas
(Contemporary Drama Service)
The First Church of Pete's Garage
(Baker's Play Publishing Co.)
Home for Christmas
(Baker's Play Publishing Co.)
Sketch Collections
Void Where Prohibited
(Baker's Play Publishing Co.)
Some Assembly Required
(Contemporary Drama Service)
Quick Skits & Discussion Starters
(co-author Chuck Bolte; Group Books)
Vantage Points
(Lillenas Publishing Co.)
Batteries Not Included
(Baker's Play Publishing Co.)
Souvenirs
(Baker's Play Publishing Co.)
Sketches of Harvest
(Baker's Play Publishing Co.)
Musicals
The Meaning of Life & Other Vanities
(co-author Tim Albritton; Baker's Play Publishing Co.)

Don't Miss the Next "Adventures in Odyssey" Book!

On this and the following pages, you'll find chapter one of
High Flyer with a Flat Tire, the next book in the "Adventures in
Odyssey" series. We hope you enjoy this preview of the book and
will then want to read the rest of the story. Don't miss it!

Mark! Hey, Mark."

Mark Prescott looked up expectantly. He had
been watching a group of boys play basketball in
McAlister Park. Like most Saturday mornings since
arriving in Odyssey, he had waited an hour for someone to
ask him to join the game. He thought the moment had
arrived.

"Mark!" Patti Eldridge called across the green expanse
of park.

Mark cringed. Patti and a girl he didn't know were rid-
ing their bikes toward him. A few weeks ago when he met
Patti, she had decided she was going to be his best friend.
Mark wasn't happy about the idea. He liked Patti well

enough, but it was embarrassing for boys to have girls as friends—even if she did a lot of boy-type things. As if to prove the point, Patti let out a wild yell, pulled the front of her bike into the air and did a wheelie down the path.

"We're going to Whit's End. You want to go?" Patti asked breathlessly as she and her friend stopped alongside Mark. "Oh, uh, Mark," Patti said, "this is Rachel Morse. Rachel, this is Mark Prescott. He's the one I told you about."

"Nice to meet you," Rachel said, hardly above a whisper. She glanced away shyly.

Mark nodded. Rachel was a chubby girl with large blue eyes and freckles dotting her round cheeks.

"So, let's go!" Patti urged.

Mark looked back at the boys and their basketball game. "Okay," he said with a shrug.

Together, they started walking across the park. Patti stopped for a moment and pushed her loose sandy hair up under her baseball cap. Mark's eye caught sight of a tiny red dot near her temple.

Patti must have noticed Mark's glance because she suddenly turned her face away. "Don't look at it! It's like a volcano."

"What?" Mark asked innocently.

"You saw it. You know. It's a zit," Patti mumbled.

She turned to Rachel. "You said nobody would notice. I told you they would."

"A zit?" Mark wasn't sure what the fuss was about. "You mean a pimple?"

"Yes, what other kind is there?" she shouted.

"I . . . I don't know." Mark felt awkward. Patti had never yelled at him like this. "What's the big deal?"

"You're a boy," Patti added. "You wouldn't understand."

Mark had to agree; he didn't want to know about Patti's pimples.

"Oh no, look who's coming," Patti moaned. "Just what I don't need."

Like cowboys on wild horses, Joe Devlin and his gang rode toward them, stirring a cloud of dust as they weaved their bicycles across each others' paths.

"Let's just walk on," Mark whispered to Patti. "Maybe they'll ride past us."

"Ha!" said Patti.

Joe and his gang surrounded Mark, Patti and Rachel.

"Well, well, well, look who's out for a Saturday morning stroll," Joe said with a sneer.

"Yeah, look who it is!" Joe's younger brother Alan piped in.

"Shut up, Alan, or I'll make you go home," Joe snapped.

Alan hung his head and closed his mouth.

Joe turned to Patti. "Where are you headed, Patti? Is it playtime at Whit's End?"

"None of your business, Joe," Patti said. "Just leave us alone."

Joe stuck his bottom lip out in a mock pout, "Aw, can't we come play with you?"

"Whit's End is open to everybody. Go on if you want," Patti replied with an air of formality.

"But we want to go with you," Joe pleaded in a whiny voice, getting a laugh from his gang.

"Get out of our way!" Patti shouted, shoving past him. She caught Joe off guard and sent his bike crashing to the ground.

Mark took a sharp, deep breath and braced himself. Rachel watched wide-eyed.

Joe quickly picked up his bike and examined it. "You're in for it now, Patti. If you hurt my new bike, I'm going to do some major damage to you."

"New bike! Is that a new bike?" Mark asked brightly.

"Yeah. A ten-speed High Flyer!" Joe announced. "It can outrun any bike in town. And there better not be any scratches on it."

"Who cares?" Patti returned. She gestured for Mark and Rachel to follow. "Come on, guys."

Joe grabbed Patti's arm and said, "I didn't give you permission to leave."

Patti tried to pull her arm away, but Joe held firm.

"Ow!" Patti cried. "Let go."

Joe laughed. "I told you I didn't give you permission to

leave. Ask for it!"

Patti struggled to get free, but Joe twisted her arm to keep his hold. Mark was about to jump into the tug-of-war when a loud, commanding voice shouted, "Let go of her!"

Startled, everyone turned to the unlikely source of the outburst. Rachel put her hand over her mouth and blushed.

Joe gave Patti a shove as he let go of her arm.

Then he glared at Rachel in a mocking way and asked, "Did you say something to me, fatso? Did a voice really come out of that barrel of blubber?"

Mark stiffened. He could think of few things more insulting than picking on someone's weight problem. Rachel lowered her head.

"Be quiet, Joe. That's no way to talk," Mark said as he stepped between Joe and Rachel.

"Stay out of this, press-snot," Joe snorted. "El blubbo can get on her bike and ride off anytime she wants, if her bike can hold all that weight. You got special shock absorbers, Rachel?"

"Shut up, Joe!" Mark shouted.

"Don't listen to this ignoramus," Patti said to Rachel.

"I'd rather be an ignoramus than a fat-oramus," Joe snickered.

"You're a jerk, Joe!" Patti said, clenching her teeth.

Mark turned to Rachel and said, "Let's go."

It was too late. Rachel's face was turning red as she

strained to keep from crying. Then large tears formed in her eyes and rolled down her cheeks. When she climbed onto her bike, she started sobbing.

"Rachel," Patti said, stepping toward her, but Rachel pushed her bike forward and took off pedaling up the path.

"Rachel!" Patti called.

Right before Rachel disappeared around the bend, Mark spotted an unfamiliar blond-haired boy on his bike. He came from behind a tree and called Rachel's name, but she didn't stop. He darted an angry look in their direction and then rode after her.

"Can't take a joke," Joe chuckled.

"You creep!" Patti roared and threw a punch at Joe. He quickly stepped back but tripped over his brother's feet and fell. Patti moved toward him with her fists clenched.

"Patti! Stop!" Mark yelled, grabbing her arm.

Her eyes ablaze, she turned; for a moment, Mark thought she was going to take a swing at him, too.

Joe sat on the grass and shouted a stream of bad names at Patti. Alan extended a hand to help him up, but Joe slapped it away.

"Get lost!" he spat and got up by himself. "Just stay out of my way."

Patti shook a finger at Joe. "Don't you ever talk to Rachel like that again."

"Why don't you try something now when I'm ready for you? Come on, tomboy. Try to fight me now."

"Don't do it," Mark said.

"That's right," Joe jeered. "Listen to your boyfriend."

"Shut up!" Patti yelled.

"Don't pay attention to him," Mark said to Patti. "My dad says that sooner or later guys like him get what they deserve."

"Guys like who?" Joe jibed.

"Guys like you who go around and start trouble for no reason," Mark returned.

Joe smiled sarcastically. "What does your dad know about anything? He's not even around. Right? That's why you and your mom came to Odyssey. I've heard all about it. Your dad doesn't like you, so he left you."

Mark threw a wild punch that grazed the side of Joe's face.

"You're going to be sorry for that," Joe shouted, tackling Mark. They fell into the dirt, tossing up a cloud of dust as they rolled over each other, struggling to pin the other one underneath. Mark swung his arms furiously, his elbow connecting with Joe's mouth. This dazed Joe enough for Mark to climb on top.

"It's the police!" someone shouted. "Police! Let's get out of here!"

Mark looked up. Joe threw Mark off his chest and gave him a blow to his cheek.

"Joe, police!" Alan cried out, pulling at his brother.

Patti grabbed Mark. "Give it up, Mark!"

Breathless, dirty and sweaty, Mark and Joe strained against the arms that held them.

"You jerk! You better hope we're never alone to finish this fight," Joe yelled. His lower lip was split and bleeding.

Mark shouted back, "Anytime, Joe! You'll get what you deserve. You'll see."

Joe and his gang jumped on their bikes and rode off. Mark glanced around for the policeman who had scared everyone away. Across the park he saw Officer Hank Snow watching them. His arms were folded, and his expression was one of silent rebuke.

"He should arrest those guys," Patti said.

Mark tried to dust himself off and then shoved his shirttail back into his jeans without much care.

"Do you still want to go to Whit's End?" Patti asked as she picked up her bike.

"No," Mark answered. "I better go home."

He took one last look at Joe, wreaking confusion among Odyssey's Main Street traffic. He was cycling recklessly between the cars. Mark wished someone would get Joe and get him good.

"Ouch!"

Mark Prescott dropped the washcloth into the bathroom sink and then stretched upward to get a better look at his face in the mirror. The red lump next to his right eye seemed to be growing.

"Oh, great," he moaned to himself, noticing the small bruise on his left cheek. "Mom's going to kill me."

He picked up the damp washcloth again, dabbed it on the sore spots and groaned from the sharp, jabbing pain. Then he ran his fingers through his dark brown hair and checked himself in the mirror one last time.

"The red lump doesn't look too bad," he assured himself.

The scratch could easily be explained to his mother. It wouldn't be an outright lie to say he had fallen, would it? He considered telling her the whole story, but he was afraid it would upset her. She had enough on her mind without worrying about Mark getting into fights. And it would hurt her if she knew the kids were saying things about Mark's dad and their separation.

Mark decided he couldn't tell her the truth. They were still the new people in town, and his mother was nervous about making a good impression. Getting in a fight, no matter whose fault it was, rarely ever left people with good impressions. Besides, Mark didn't want to get punished.

He threw the washcloth into the hamper, went to his room and put on a clean shirt and a favorite pair of jeans.

Just like new, he thought as he walked down the stairs.

Jumping the bottom two steps, he could see his mother through the living room doorway. She was sitting on the love seat, her hands knotted in her lap. Her glance caught Mark's.

"Come in here, son," she called with a worried tone that Mark knew well.

As he stepped through the doorway into the living room, he saw why. A stern-looking woman was sitting on the couch, holding a slashed bicycle tire that looked like chopped black licorice.

Joe Devlin was sitting next to her.